W9-BMW-552

SEARCH AND RESCUE!

Random House 🏠 New York

Thomas the Tank Engine & Friends™

CREATED BY BRITT ALLCROFT

Based on The Railway Series by The Reverend W Awdry.
© 2012 Gullane (Thomas) LLC.
Thomas the Tank Engine & Friends and Thomas & Friends are trademarks of Gullane (Thomas) Limited.
HIT and the HIT Entertainment logo are trademarks of HIT Entertainment Limited.
All rights reserved. Published in the United States by Random House Children's Books, a division of Random House, Inc., 1745 Broadway, New York, NY 10019, and in Canada by Random House of Canada Limited, Toronto. Random House and the colophon are registered trademarks of Random House, Inc.

ISBN: 978-0-307-93029-3

www.randomhouse.com/kids   www.thomasandfriends.com

MANUFACTURED IN MALAYSIA

10 9 8 7 6 5 4 3 2 1

HIT entertainment

It is early in the morning on the Island of Sodor. There was a big storm last night. Thomas is very busy clearing tracks and delivering supplies.

Thomas will be busy the whole day, and he needs his friends to help. Can you find Percy?

The big storm damaged the sign on the Sodor
Search and Rescue Center. Sir Topham Hatt needs
Thomas to go to the Docks to pick up a new sign
for the center.

Where is Sir Topham Hatt? Will you help
Thomas find him?

Thomas hurries to the Docks. They are
bustling with activity.

"I have a special job to do," he peeps to
Spencer.

"If it were truly special, I would be doing
it," Spencer steams. "Now out of my way,
please. I have a job to do for the Duke and
Duchess of Boxford."

Will you help Cranky find the crate
for Thomas to deliver?

Spencer speeds away from the Docks.
He races around a sharp turn too late to see
messy trucks filled with garbage on the track
ahead. Spencer tries to stop, but the tracks
are slippery.
CRASH!

News of Spencer's accident spreads
quickly. Who tells Thomas?

Thomas knows he has a special job to do, but he thinks he should try to help Spencer. He quickly collects some workers and goes to the site of the accident.

Will you help the workers get ready to clear the tracks?

Rocky is ready to help Spencer
get to the Steamworks.

Oh, no! One of the workers is hurt. Can you help Harold rescue him?

Sir Topham Hatt is waiting for Thomas at the Sodor Search and Rescue Center.

"It's important to do our jobs," says Sir Topham Hatt. "But it's also important to help our friends when they're in trouble. Thomas, you are a Really Useful Engine and a very good friend."

Thomas puffs with pride.

Can you put the new sign on the
Sodor Search and Rescue Center?

The busy day is over, and Thomas rolls back to Tidmouth Sheds for a well-deserved rest. He is happy that he has been Really Useful, and he is happy to have so many helpful friends.